ODD SOCKS!

Published by TROIKA BOOKS

First published 2016

Troika Books
Well House, Green Lane, Ardleigh CO7 7PD
www.troikabooks.com

Text copyright © Neal Zetter 2016
Illustrations copyright © Chris White 2016

The moral rights of the author and illustrator have been asserted

A CIP catalogue record for this book is available from the British Library

ISBN 978-1-909991-41-5

1 2 3 4 5 6 7 8 9 10

Printed in Poland

ODD SOCKS!

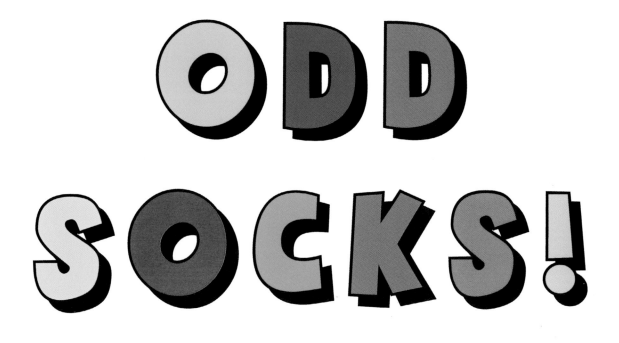

Neal Zetter

Illustrated by

Chris White

troika books

Odd socks
are all
I ever wear

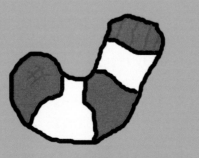

Which one vanished in the night?

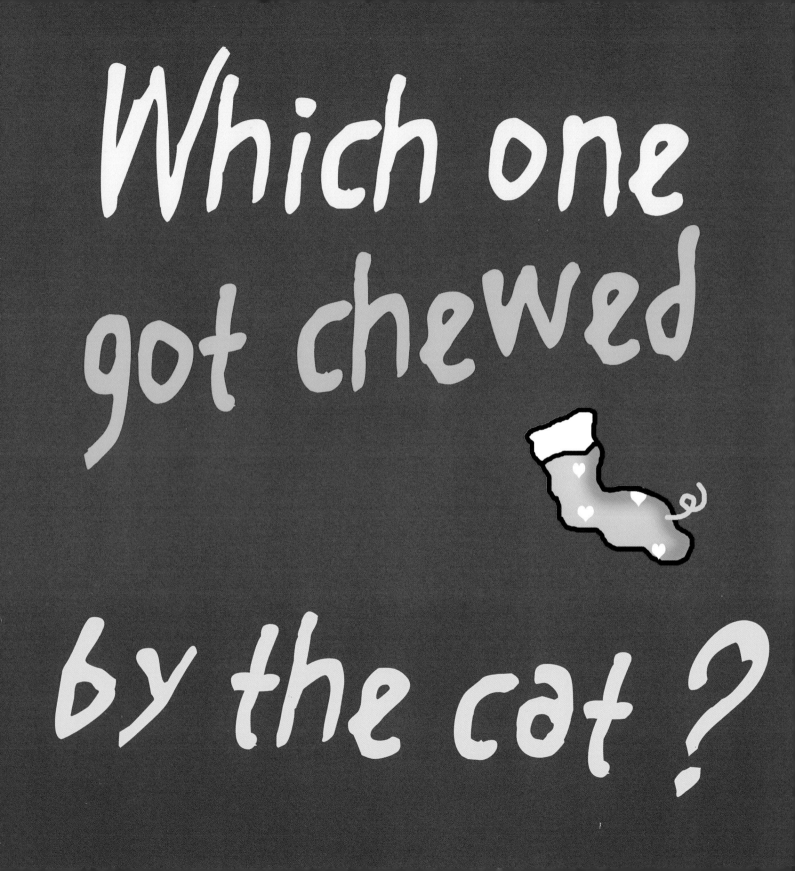

Which one

disappeared

from

town?

Which  one did Mum set alight?

Which one was advertised and sold?

Which one
hid inside
my shoe?

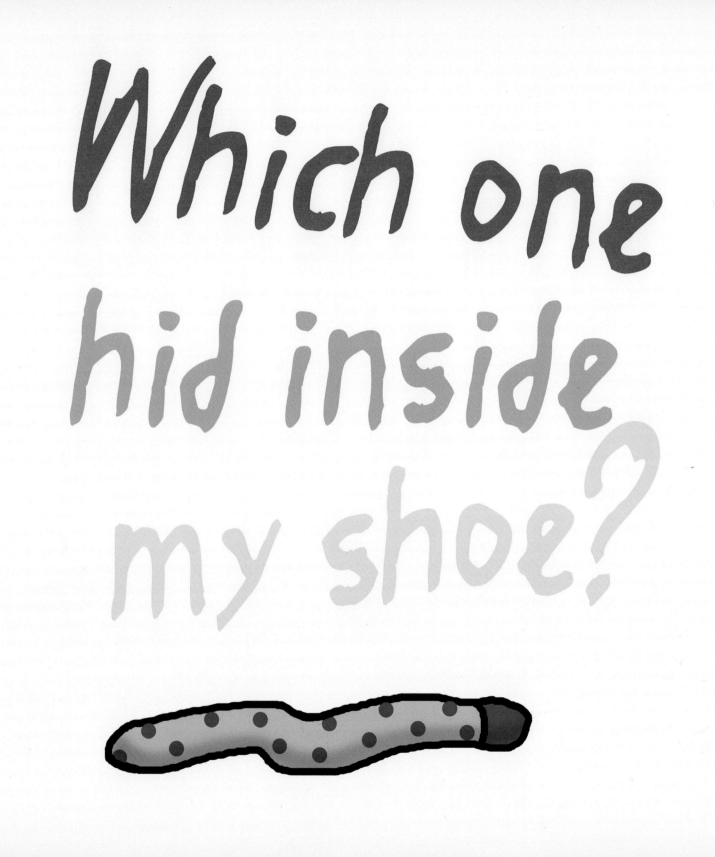

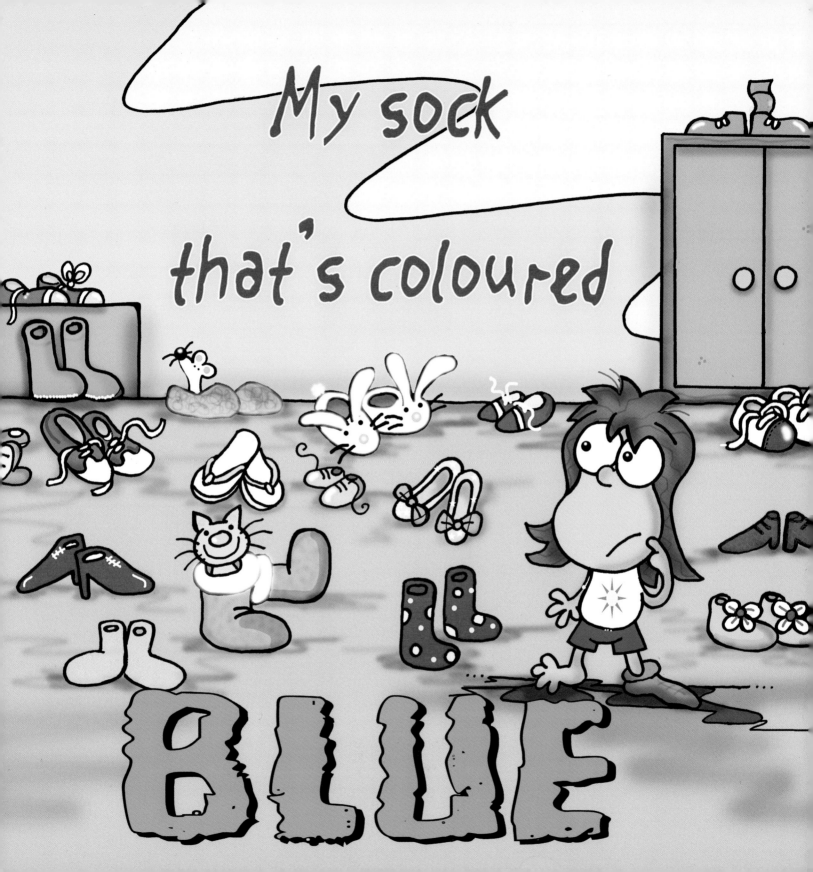

Odd socks are all
I ever wear